# Cindy the Cicada

## By Carol Petraitis

Illustrated by Candice Kamperin

This book is dedicated to the
staff and students of
Calvert Country School, Prince Frederick, MD.

It has been 17 years since Cindy hatched from an egg and burrowed deep underground.

Cindy spent the last few weeks tunneling her way up toward the earth's surface. She noticed a light up ahead. She grew tired when she felt the warmth of the sun on her body. Cindy knew she could not stop now. She had a mission to complete above ground.

3

Cindy started climbing the nearest object. Halfway up, she decided it was time to molt her shell.

As Cindy climbed out of her shell, she felt the warm spring air. As the heat warmed her body, her wings began to unfold. Soon she would be ready to fly.

Cindy was unsure of where she was. Suddenly, she felt a burning sensation. All of her senses told her to fly away from the hot surface. She spread her wings and soared into the air. Extremely unsteady, Cindy flew straight into a spider's web. She struggled and struggled, but could not free herself. The nearby spider was thinking that the cicada would make a delicious meal.

Suddenly, a strong wind blew and destroyed the spider's web. Cindy fell to the ground. The remains of the sticky spider's web prevented Cindy from flying away.

A black cat saw the struggling cicada and quickly decided it would make a tasty treat. The cat grabbed Cindy with his mouth and trotted for home.

All of a sudden, the cat noticed a dog running towards him. The cat immediately dropped Cindy and ran up a nearby tree.

Unharmed, Cindy flew into the air. Just then, a bird flew down and snatched Cindy with her beak. The bird thought the cicada would make a perfect dinner for her babies anxiously waiting back at her nest.

Cindy fluttered and fluttered to free herself. Suddenly, there was the sound of thunder, and it began to rain. It rained so hard that the bird dropped Cindy as she tried to remain steady in flight.

Cindy landed upon a tree branch.
Totally exhausted, she fell asleep.

That evening, Cindy awoke to the most beautiful sound she has ever heard. It was the singing of a male cicada searching for a mate. Cindy realized that she must find him.

Cindy followed the sound of the male cicada's sweet song to a huge oak tree. She discovered Charlie perched on a branch.

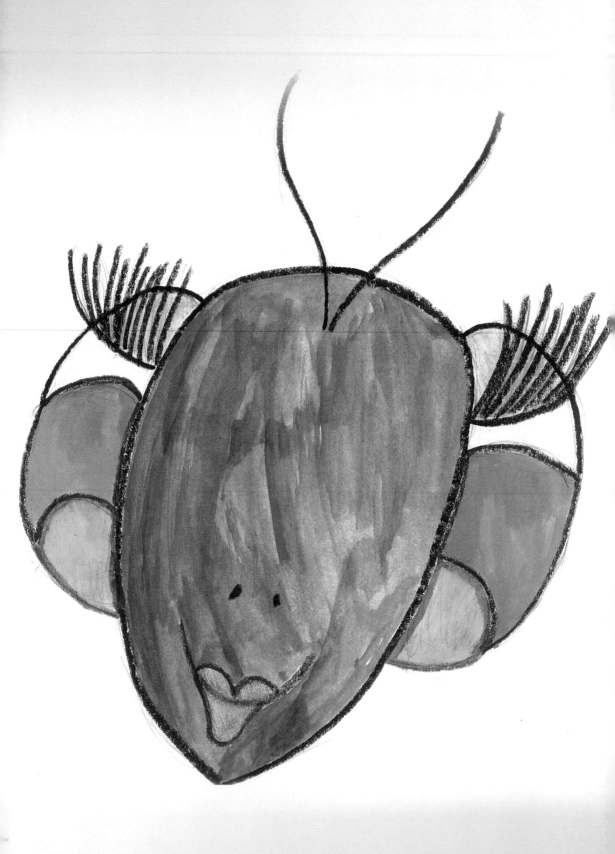

When Charlie looked into Cindy's beautiful reddish-orange eyes, he knew that he had found his mate. For the next ten days, Cindy and Charlie did everything together.

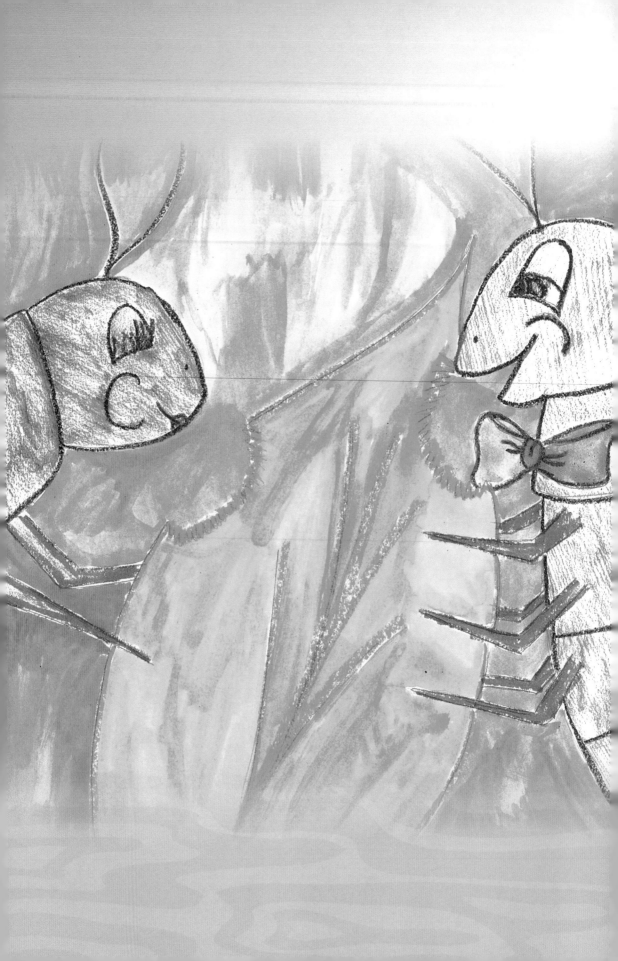

They ate their meals together.

They played tag in the sky.

They danced to Charlie's
beautiful singing.

On the tenth day, Charlie
and Cindy searched for the
perfect tree where Cindy
would lay her eggs.

After making sure the eggs were safe, Cindy and Charlie happily flew away. They had completed their mission together.

# The End

Made in the USA
Charleston, SC
13 November 2015